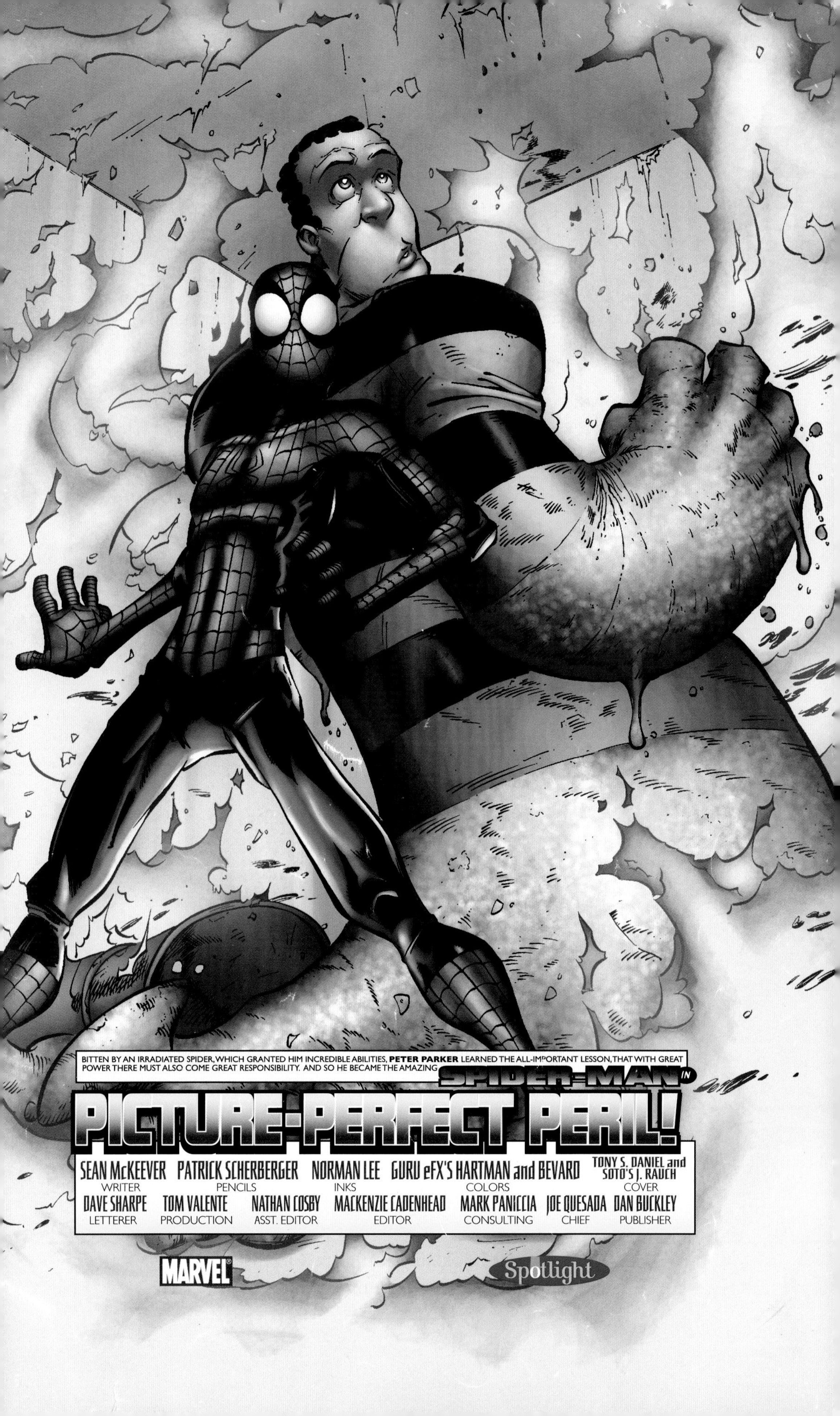
BITTEN BY AN IRRADIATED SPIDER, WHICH GRANTED HIM INCREDIBLE ABILITIES, PETER PARKER LEARNED THE ALL-IMPORTANT LESSON, THAT WITH GREAT POWER THERE MUST ALSO COME GREAT RESPONSIBILITY. AND SO HE BECAME THE AMAZING
SPIDER-MAN IN
PICTURE-PERFECT PERIL!
SEAN McKEEVER WRITER
PATRICK SCHERBERGER PENCILS
NORMAN LEE INKS
GURU eFX'S HARTMAN and BEVARD COLORS
TONY S. DANIEL and SOTO'S J. RAUCH COVER
DAVE SHARPE LETTERER
TOM VALENTE PRODUCTION
NATHAN COSBY ASST. EDITOR
MACKENZIE CADENHEAD EDITOR
MARK PANICCIA CONSULTING
JOE QUESADA CHIEF
DAN BUCKLEY PUBLISHER
MARVEL®
Spotlight

VISIT US AT
www.abdopublishing.com

Spotlight library bound edition © 2007. Spotlight is a division of ABDO Publishing Company, Edina, Minnesota.

Cataloging Data

McKeever, Sean
    Picture-perfect peril! / Sean McKeever, writer ; Patrick Scherberger, pencils ; Norman Lee, inks -- Library bound ed.
        p. cm. -- (Spider-Man)
    Summary: Introduces readers of all ages to some of the greatest stories of the legendary Marvel Universe.
    "Marvel age"--Cover.
    Revision of the October 2005 issue of Marvel adventures Spider-Man.
    ISBN-13: 978-1-59961-212-6 (Reinforced Library Bound Edition)
    ISBN-10: 1-59961-212-7 (Reinforced Library Bound Edition)
        1. Spider-Man (Fictitious character)--Fiction. 2. Comic books, strips, etc.--Fiction. 3. Graphic novels. I. Title. II. Series.

741.5dc22

All Spotlight books are reinforced library binding and manufactured in the United States of America

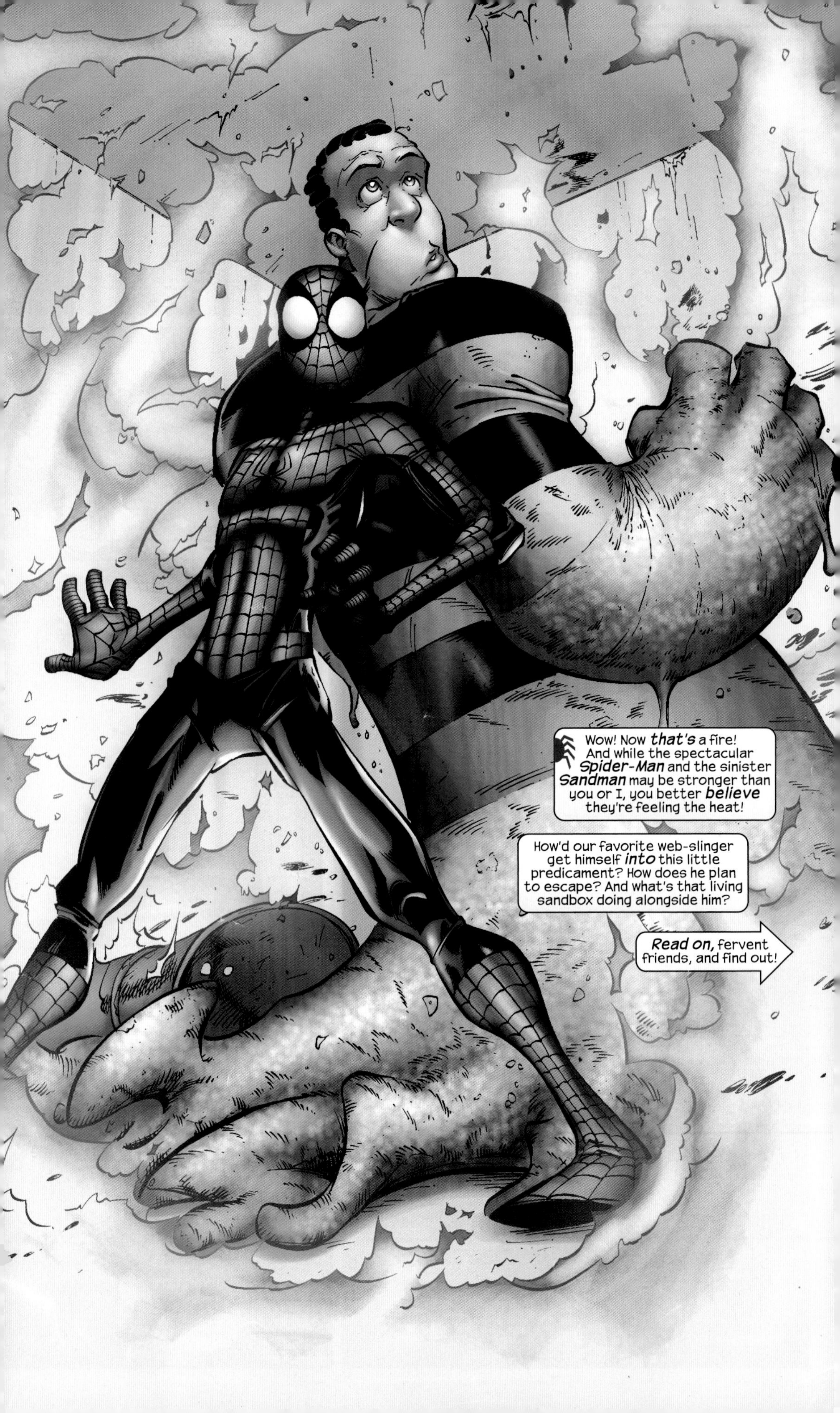
Wow! Now that's a fire! And while the spectacular Spider-Man and the sinister Sandman may be stronger than you or I, you better believe they're feeling the heat!
How'd our favorite web-slinger get himself into this little predicament? How does he plan to escape? And what's that living sandbox doing alongside him?
Read on, fervent friends, and find out!

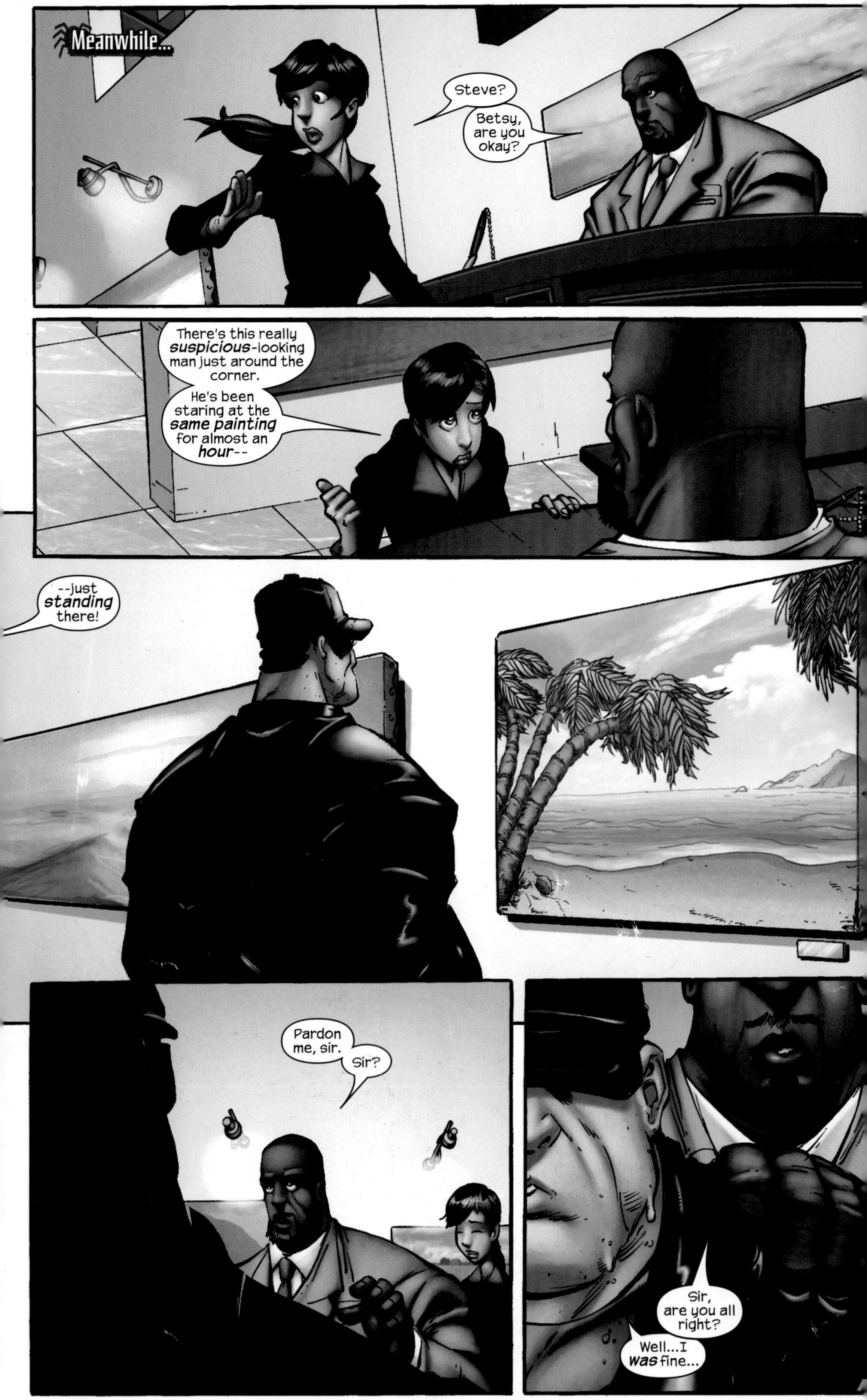
Meanwhile...
Steve?
Betsy, are you okay?
There's this really *suspicious*-looking man just around the corner.
He's been staring at the *same painting* for almost an *hour*--
--just *standing* there!
Pardon me, sir.
Sir?
Sir, are you all right?
Well...I *was* fine...

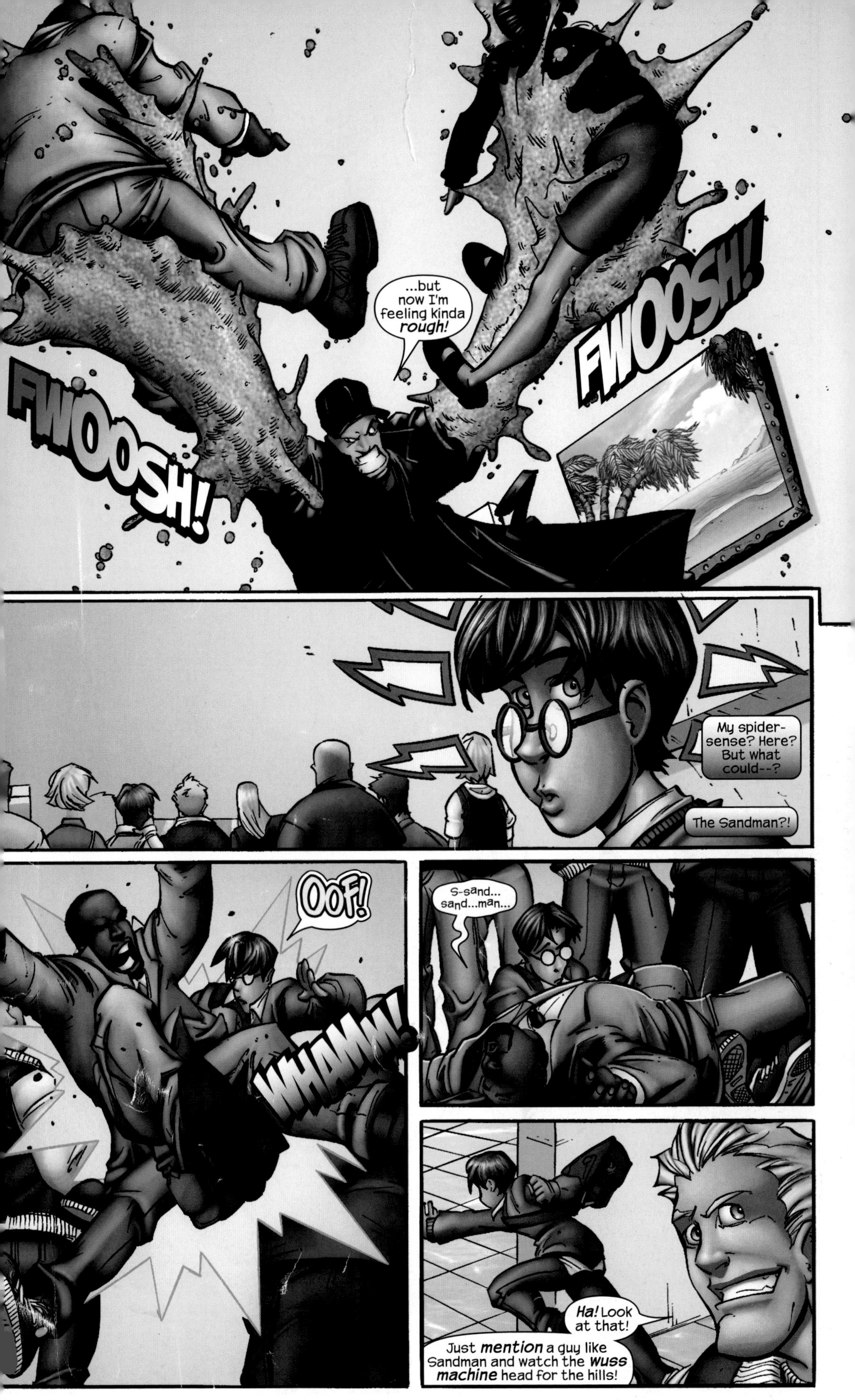
...but now I'm feeling kinda rough!
FWOOSH!
FWOOSH!
My spider-sense? Here? But what could--?
The Sandman?!
OOF!
WHAMM!
S-sand... sand...man...
Ha! Look at that!
Just mention a guy like Sandman and watch the wuss machine head for the hills!

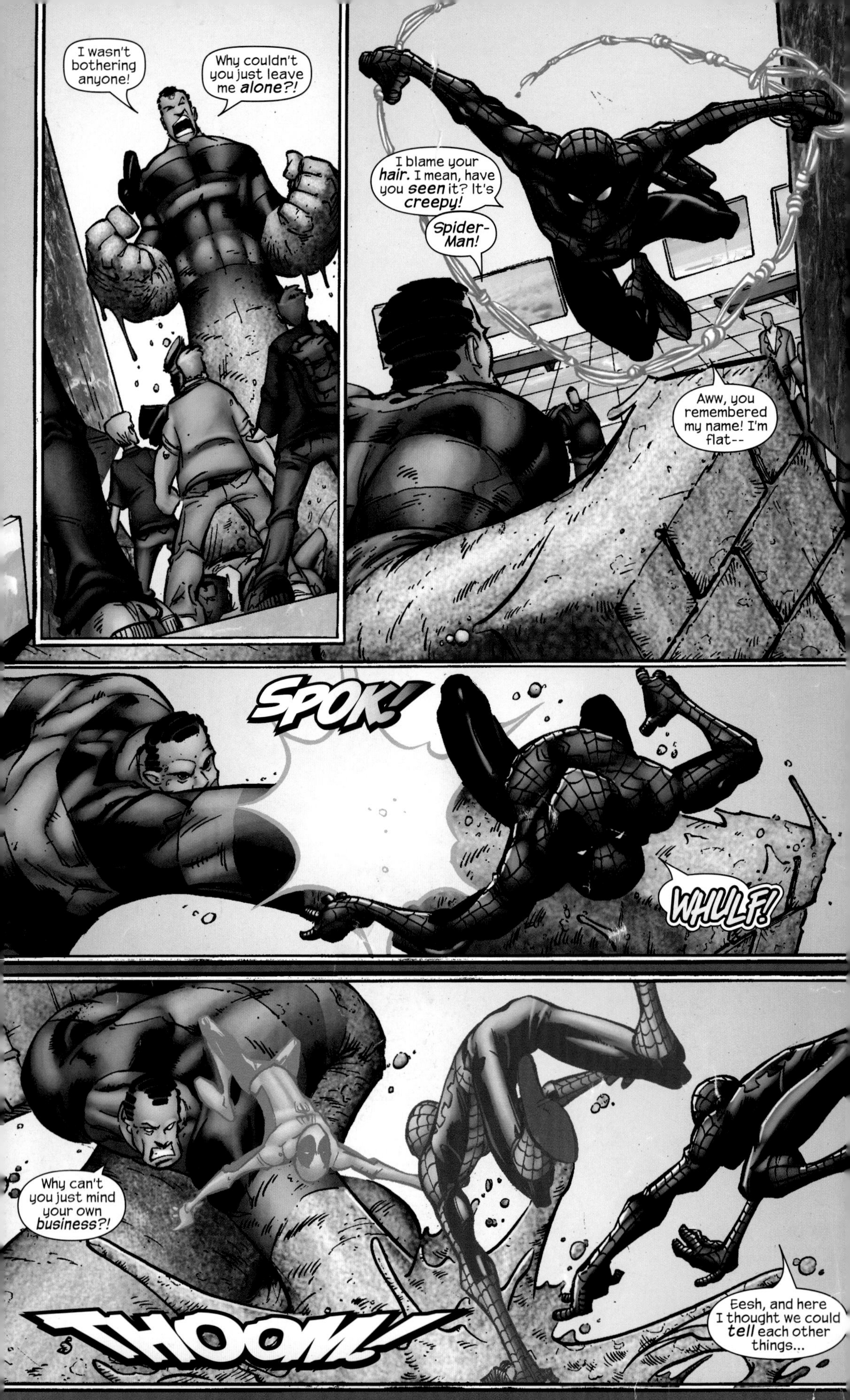
I wasn't bothering anyone!
Why couldn't you just leave me *alone*?!
I blame your *hair.* I mean, have you *seen* it? It's *creepy!*
Spider-Man!
Aww, you remembered my name! I'm flat--
SPOK!
WHULF!
Why can't you just mind your own *business*?!
THOOM!
Eesh, and here I thought we could *tell* each other things...

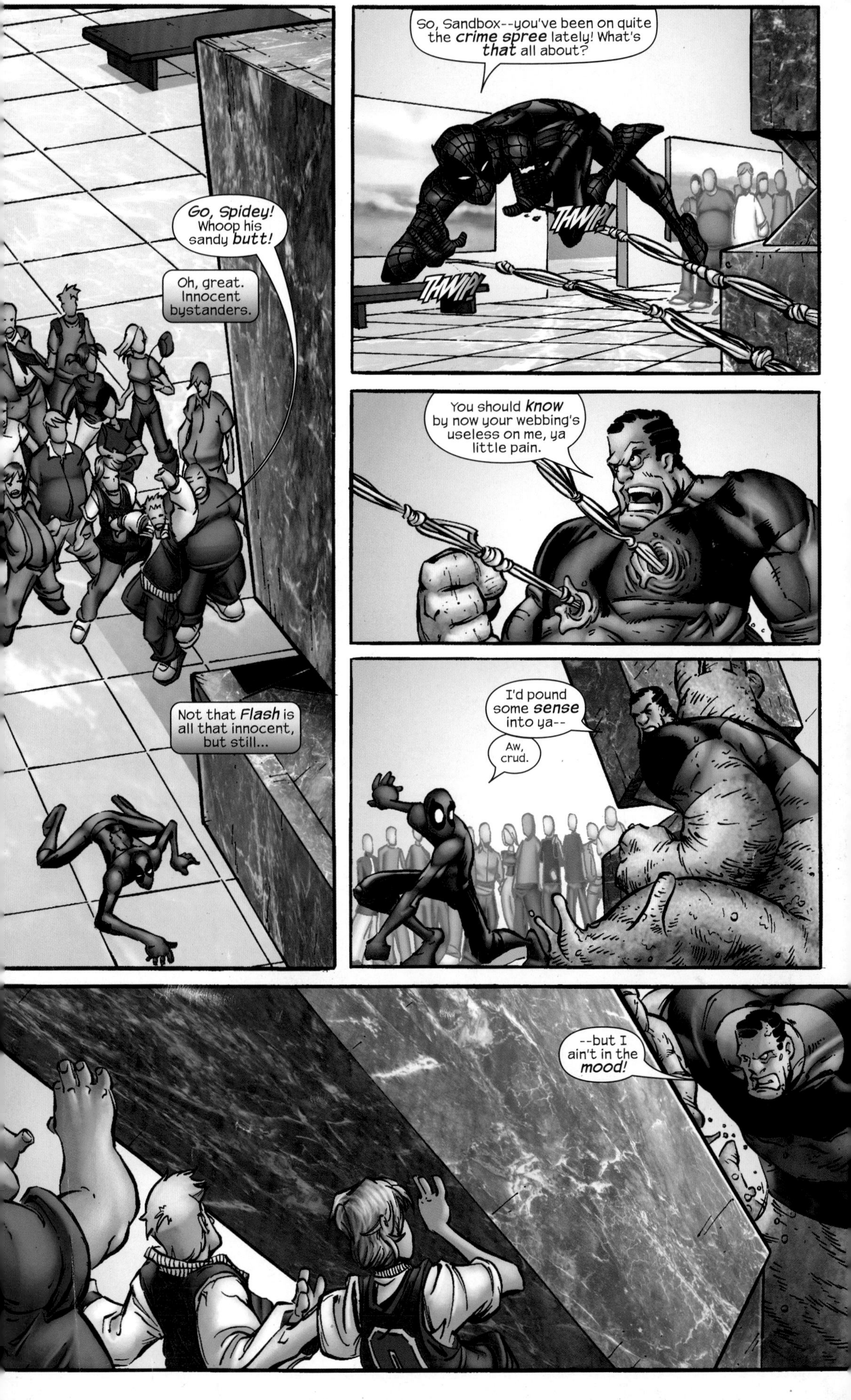
Go, Spidey! Whoop his sandy butt!
Oh, great. Innocent bystanders.
Not that Flash is all that innocent, but still...
So, Sandbox--you've been on quite the crime spree lately! What's that all about?
THWIP!
THWIP!
You should know by now your webbing's useless on me, ya little pain.
I'd pound some sense into ya--
Aw, crud.
--but I ain't in the mood!

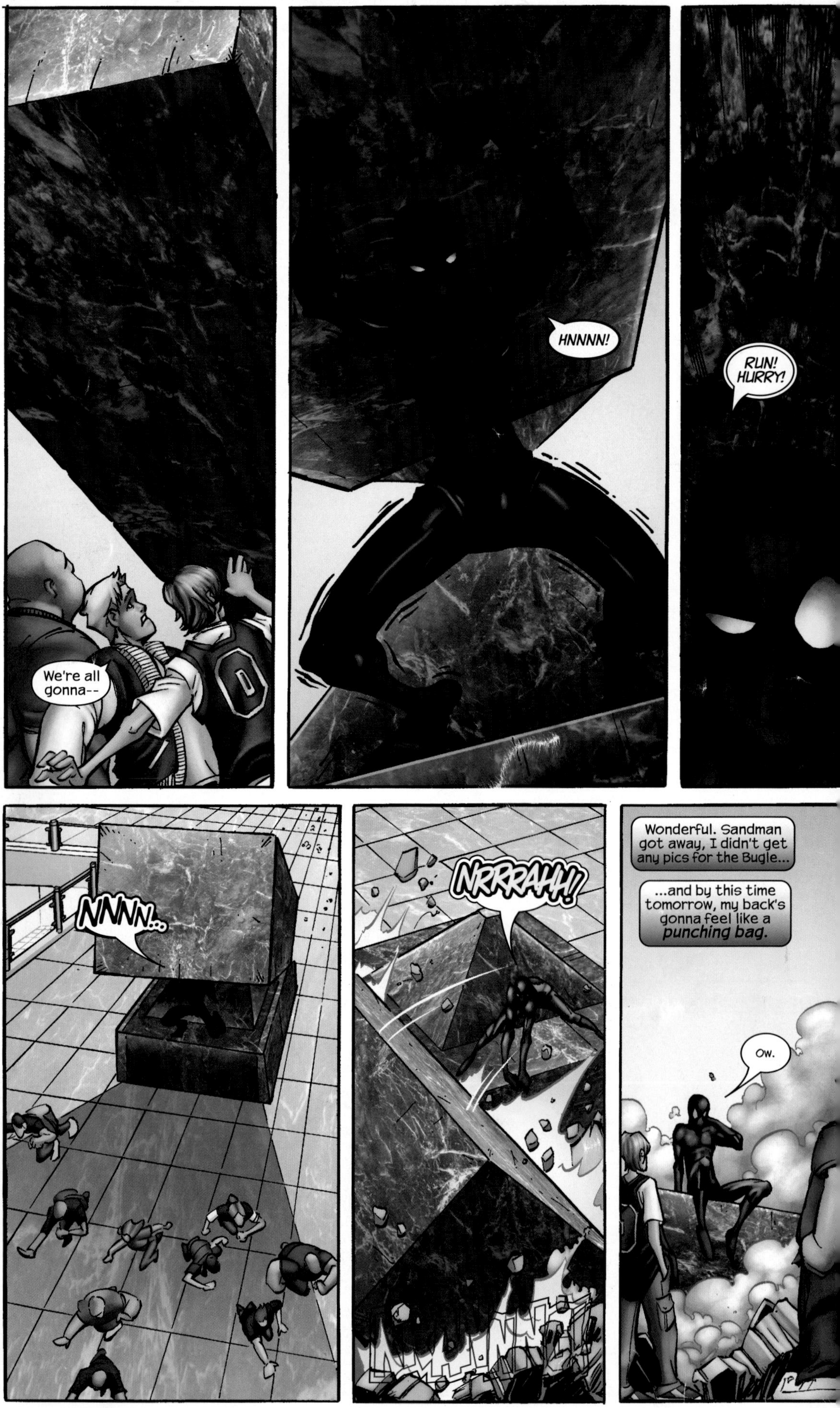
We're all gonna--
HNNNN!
RUN! HURRY!
NNNN...
NRRRAHH!
Wonderful. Sandman got away, I didn't get any pics for the Bugle...
...and by this time tomorrow, my back's gonna feel like a punching bag.
Ow.

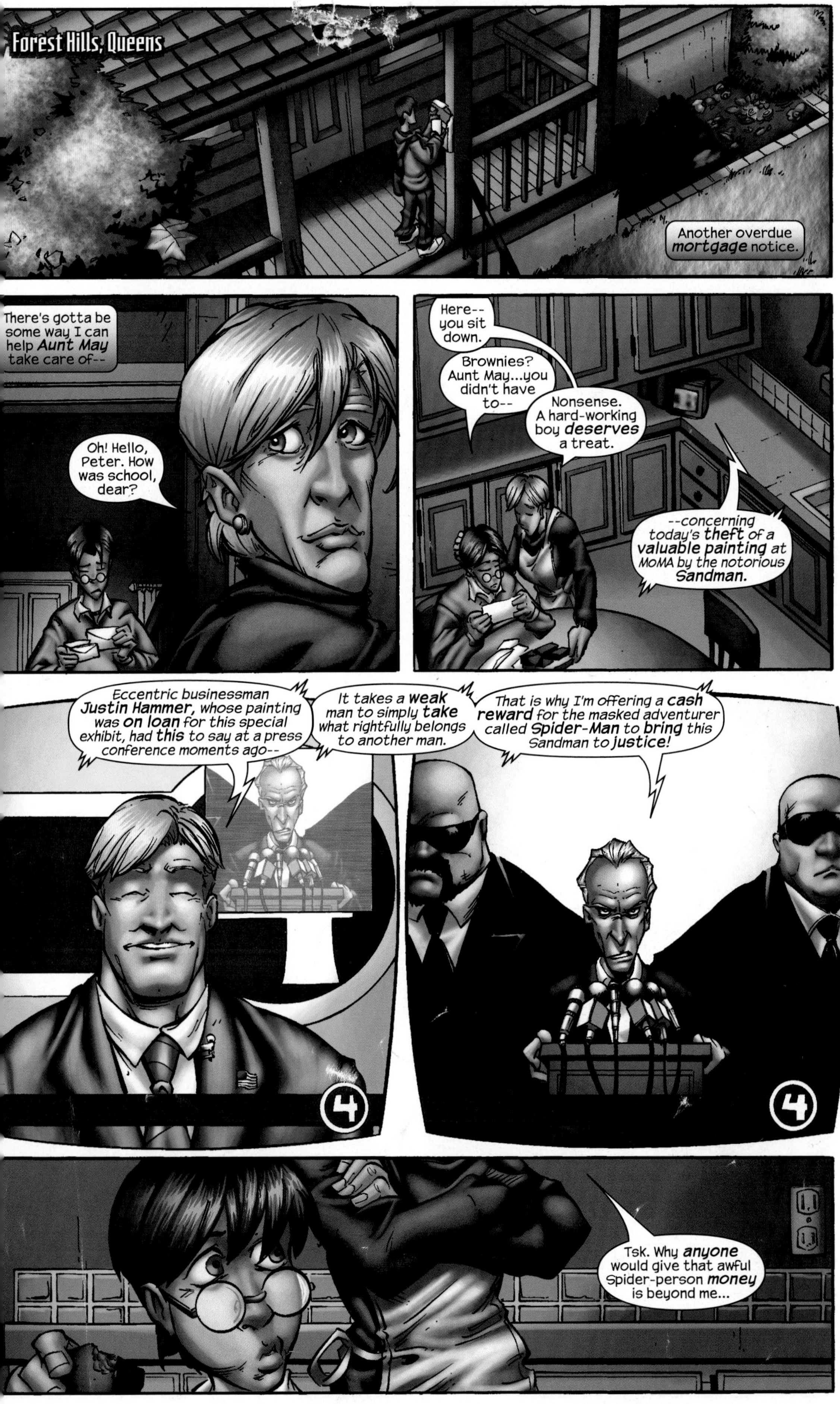
Forest Hills, Queens
Another overdue mortgage notice.
There's gotta be some way I can help Aunt May take care of--
Oh! Hello, Peter. How was school, dear?
Here-- you sit down.
Brownies? Aunt May...you didn't have to--
Nonsense. A hard-working boy deserves a treat.
--concerning today's theft of a valuable painting at MoMA by the notorious Sandman.
Eccentric businessman Justin Hammer, whose painting was on loan for this special exhibit, had this to say at a press conference moments ago--
It takes a weak man to simply take what rightfully belongs to another man.
That is why I'm offering a cash reward for the masked adventurer called Spider-Man to bring this Sandman to justice!
Tsk. Why anyone would give that awful Spider-person money is beyond me...

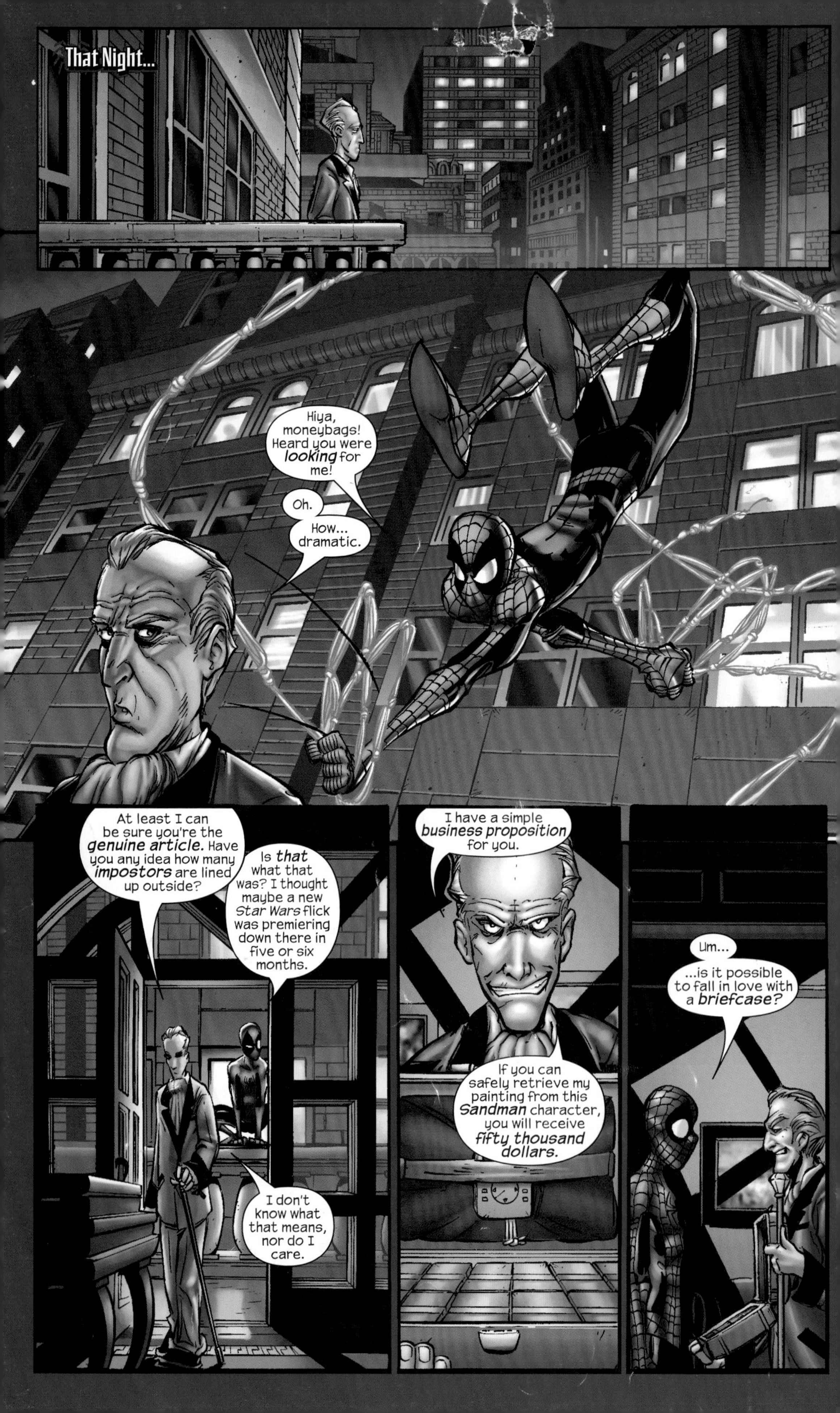

That Night...
Hiya, moneybags! Heard you were *looking* for me!
Oh.
How... dramatic.
At least I can be sure you're the **genuine article.** Have you any idea how many **impostors** are lined up outside?
Is *that* what that was? I thought maybe a new *Star Wars* flick was premiering down there in five or six months.
I don't know what that means, nor do I care.
I have a simple **business proposition** for you.
If you can safely retrieve my painting from this **Sandman** character, you will receive **fifty thousand dollars.**
Um...
...is it possible to fall in love with a **briefcase?**

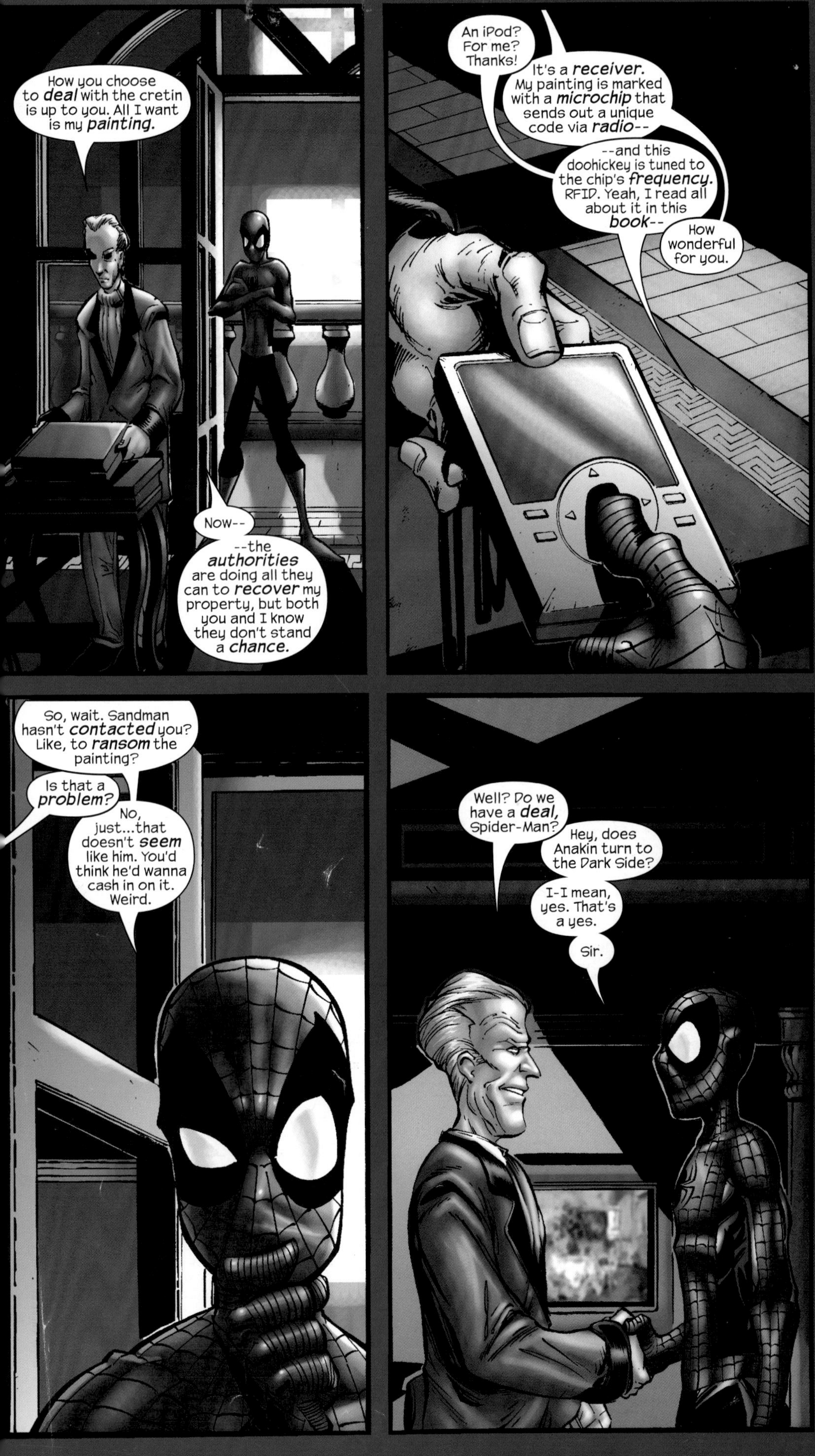
How you choose to *deal* with the cretin is up to you. All I want is my *painting*.
Now--
--the *authorities* are doing all they can to *recover* my property, but both you and I know they don't stand a *chance*.
An iPod? For me? Thanks!
It's a *receiver*. My painting is marked with a *microchip* that sends out a unique code via *radio*--
--and this doohickey is tuned to the chip's *frequency*. RFID. Yeah, I read all about it in this *book*--
How wonderful for you.
So, wait. Sandman hasn't *contacted* you? Like, to *ransom* the painting?
Is that a *problem*?
No, just...that doesn't *seem* like him. You'd think he'd wanna cash in on it. Weird.
Well? Do we have a *deal*, Spider-Man?
Hey, does Anakin turn to the Dark Side?
I-I mean, yes. That's a yes.
Sir.

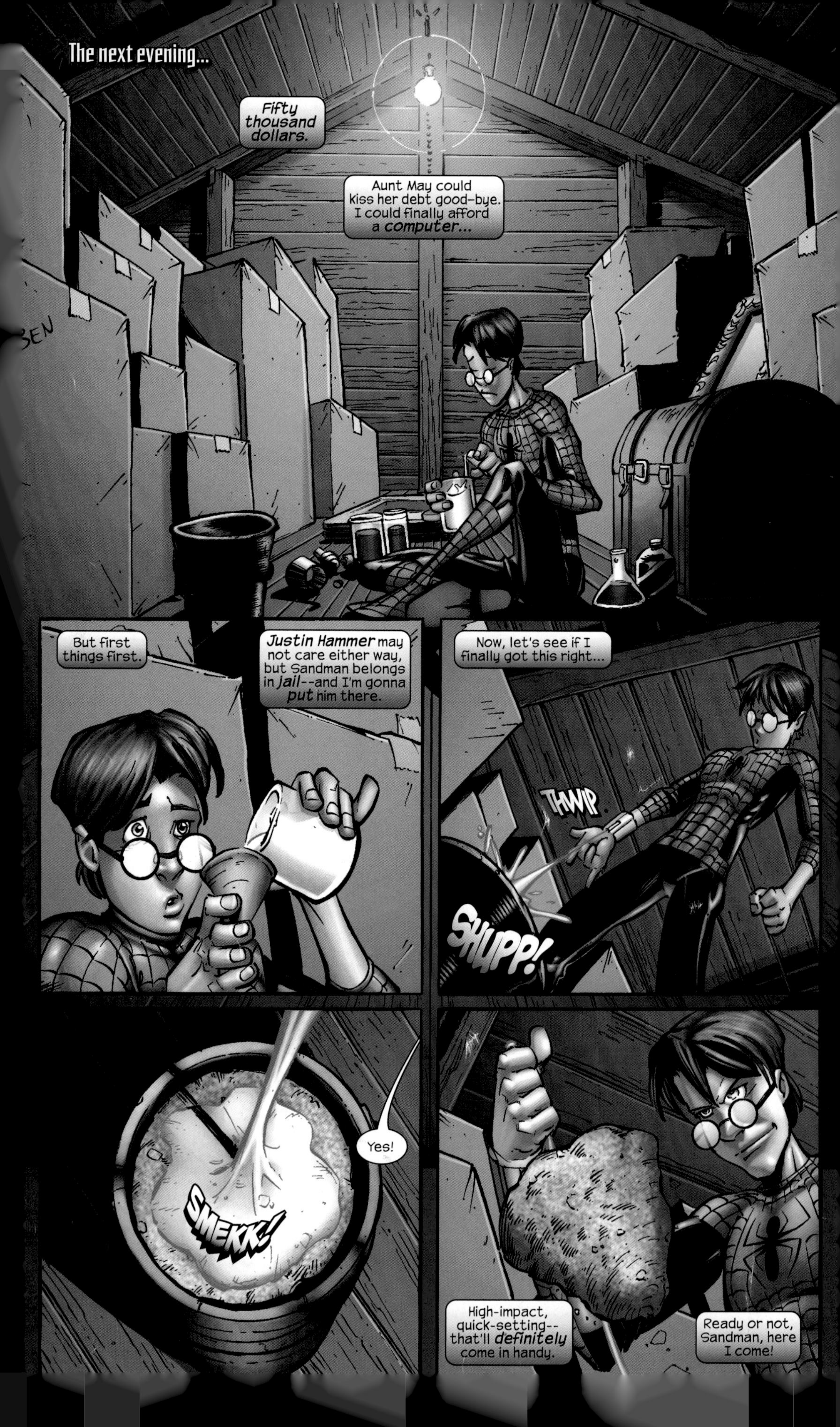
The next evening...
Fifty thousand dollars.
Aunt May could kiss her debt good-bye. I could finally afford a computer...
BEN
But first things first.
Justin Hammer may not care either way, but Sandman belongs in jail--and I'm gonna put him there.
Now, let's see if I finally got this right...
THWIP
SHUPP!
SMEKK!
Yes!
High-impact, quick-setting--that'll definitely come in handy.
Ready or not, Sandman, here I come!

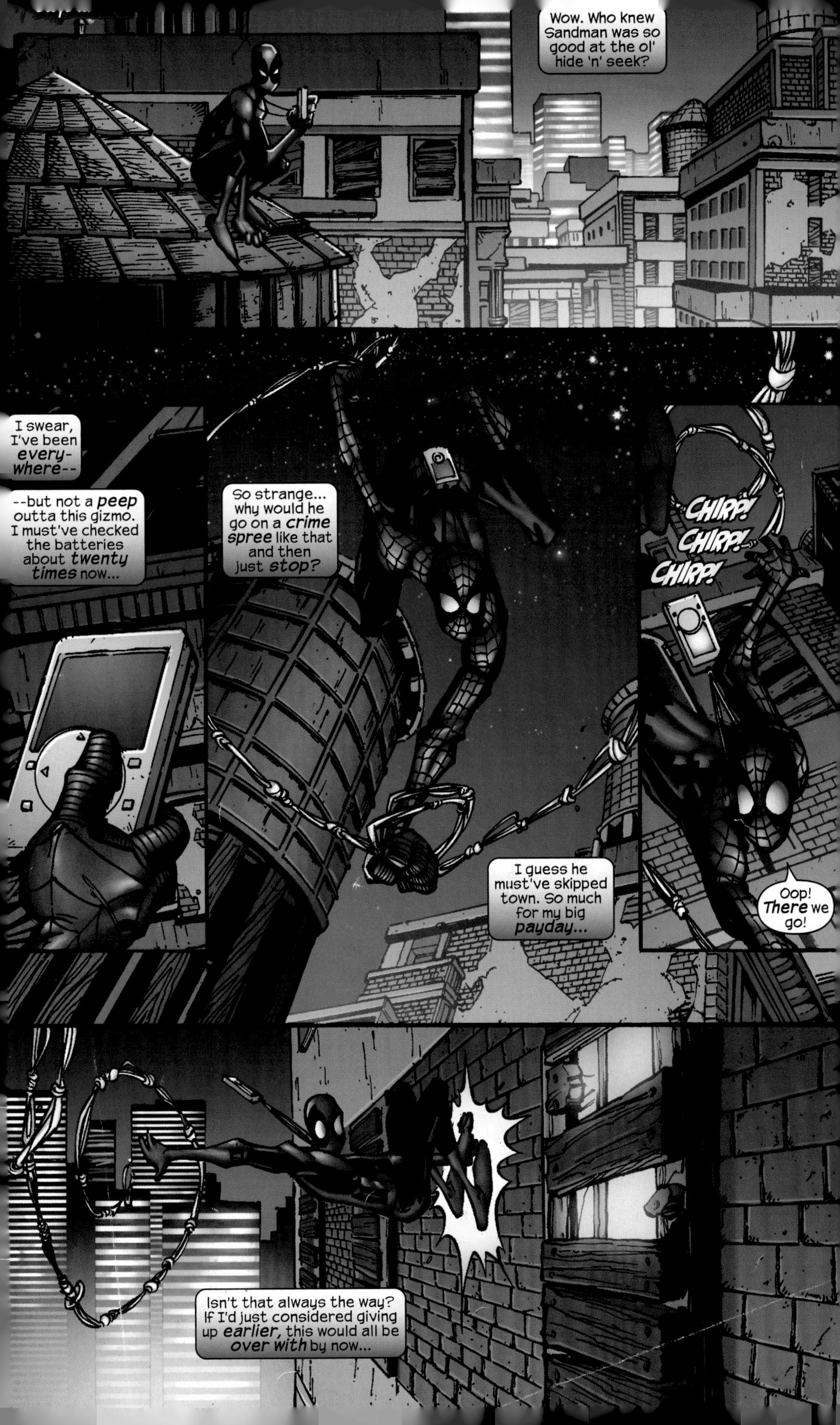
Wow. Who knew Sandman was so good at the ol' hide 'n' seek?
I swear, I've been every-where--
--but not a peep outta this gizmo. I must've checked the batteries about twenty times now...
So strange... why would he go on a crime spree like that and then just stop?
CHIRP! CHIRP! CHIRP!
I guess he must've skipped town. So much for my big payday...
Oop! There we go!
Isn't that always the way? If I'd just considered giving up earlier, this would all be over with by now...

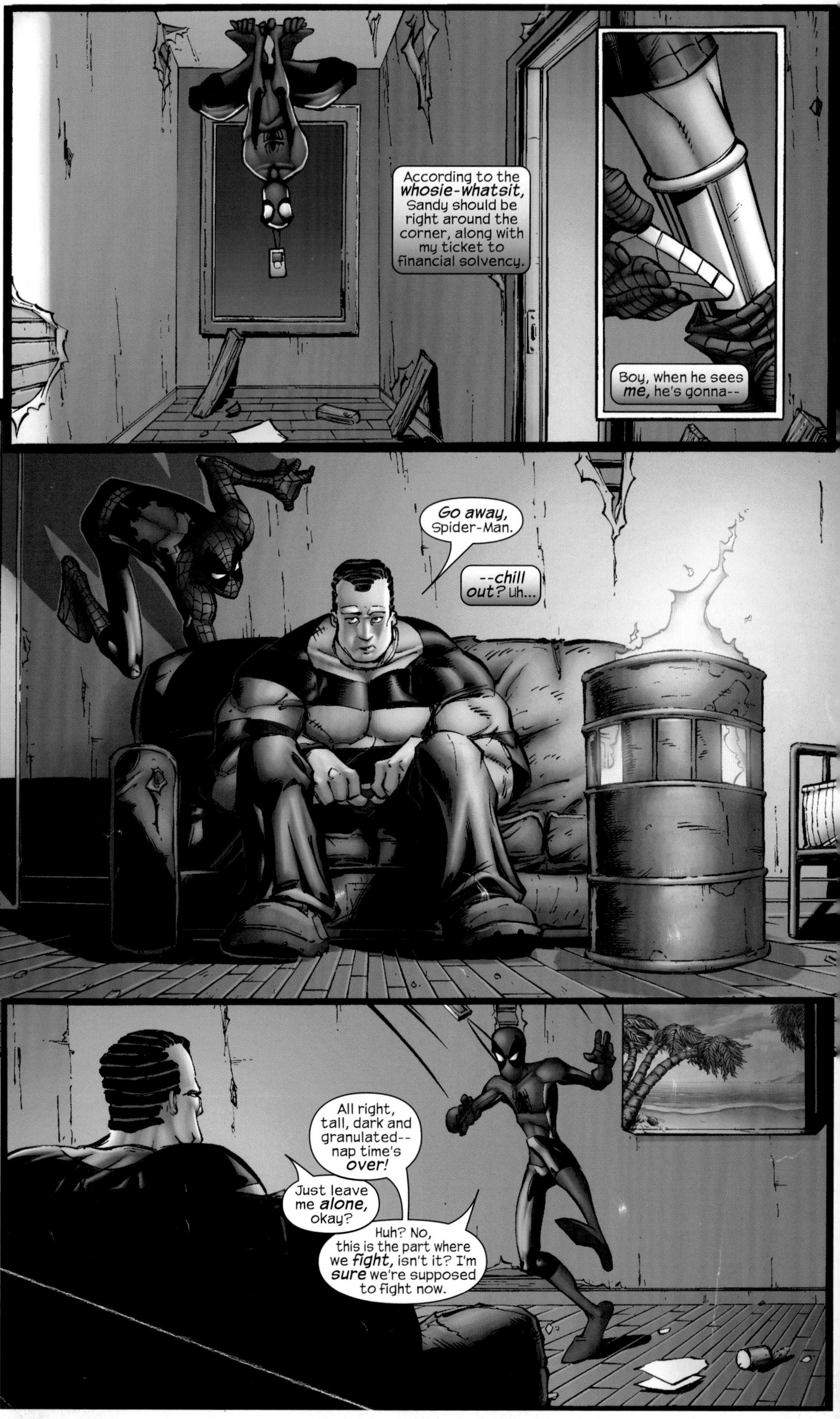
According to the whosie-whatsit, Sandy should be right around the corner, along with my ticket to financial solvency.
Boy, when he sees me, he's gonna--
Go away, Spider-Man.
--chill out? uh...
All right, tall, dark and granulated-- nap time's over!
Just leave me alone, okay?
Huh? No, this is the part where we fight, isn't it? I'm sure we're supposed to fight now.

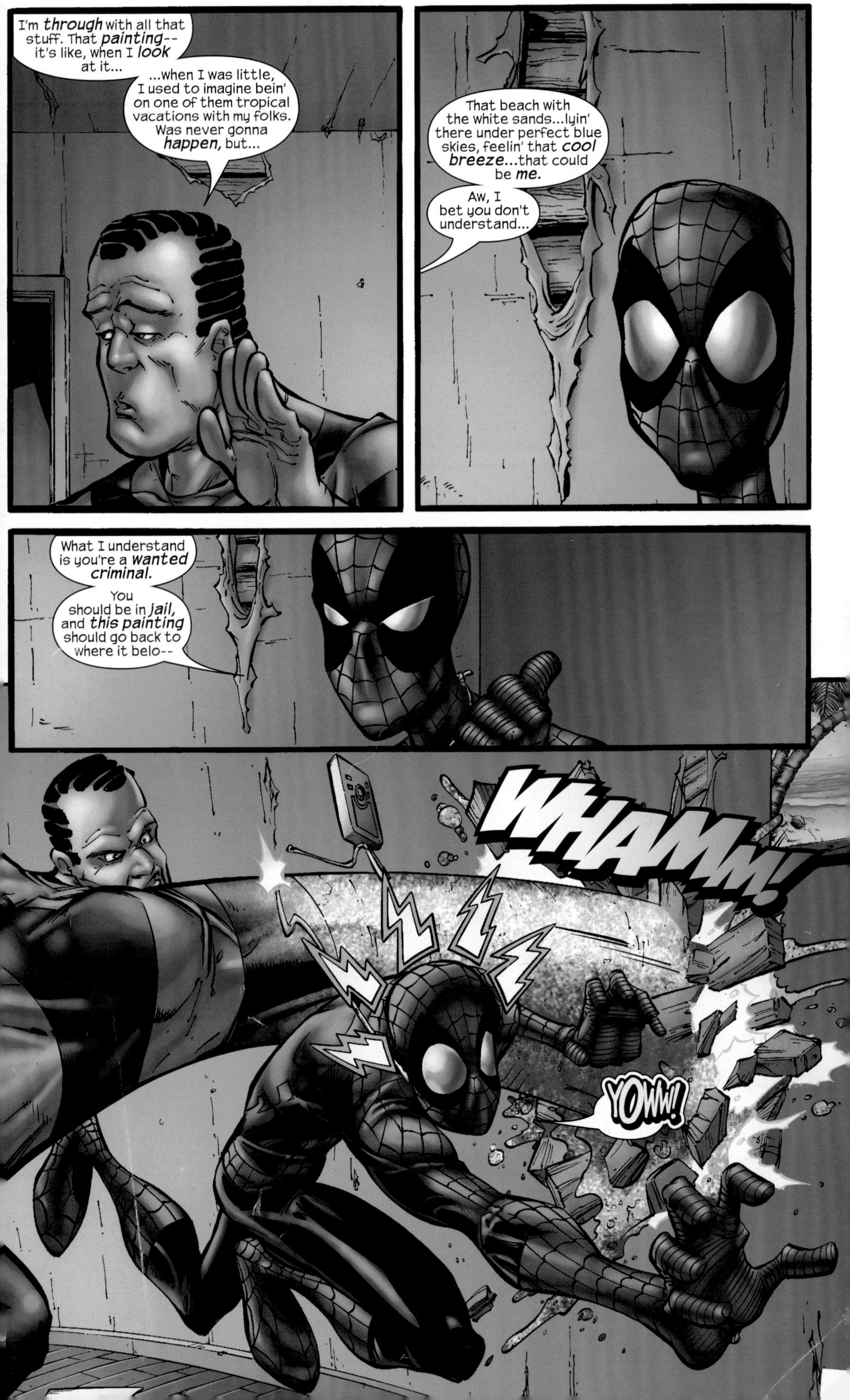

I'm through with all that stuff. That painting-- it's like, when I look at it...
...when I was little, I used to imagine bein' on one of them tropical vacations with my folks. Was never gonna happen, but...
That beach with the white sands...lyin' there under perfect blue skies, feelin' that cool breeze...that could be me.
Aw, I bet you don't understand...
What I understand is you're a wanted criminal.
You should be in jail, and this painting should go back to where it belo--
WHAMM!
YOWW!

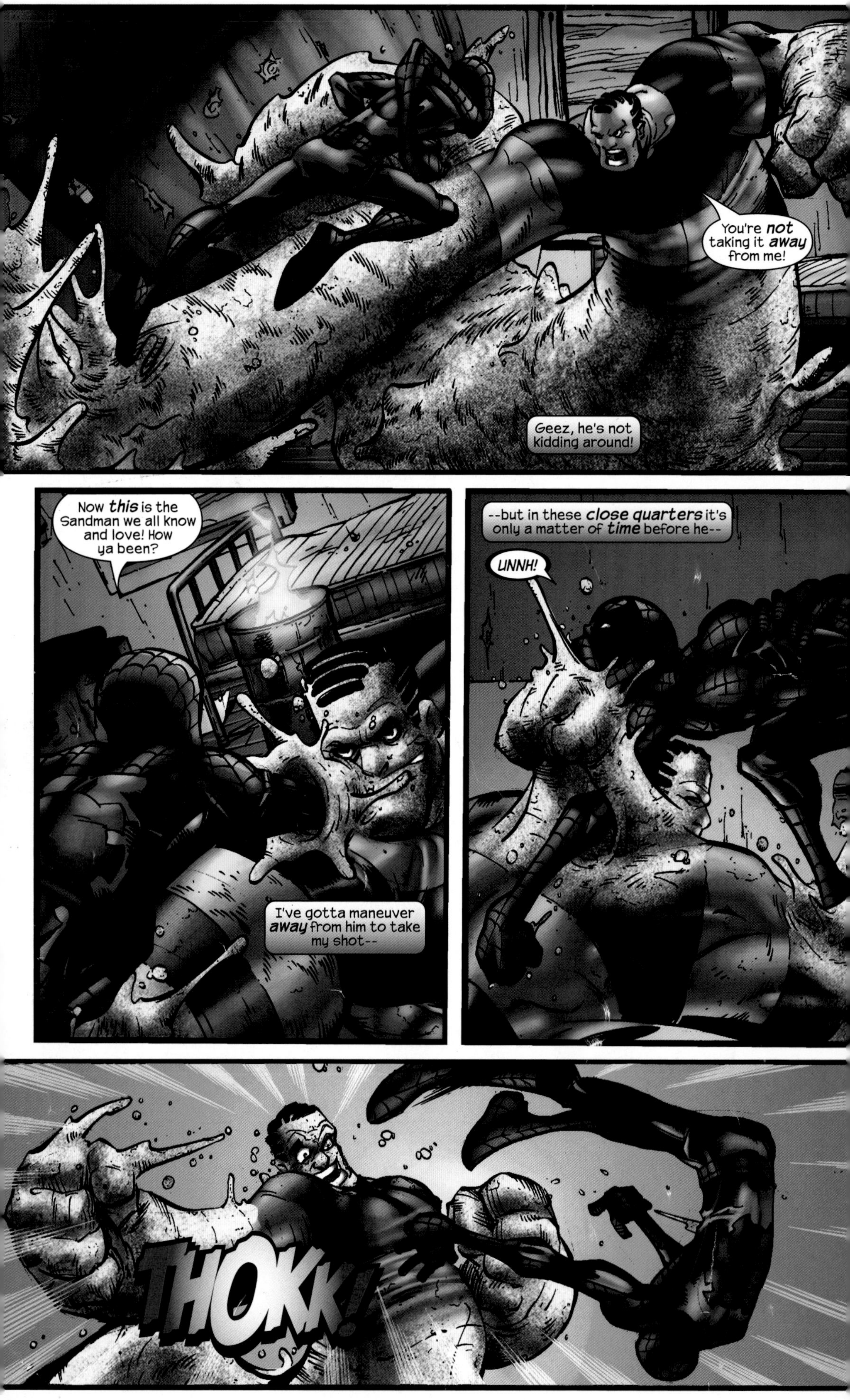
You're not taking it away from me!
Geez, he's not kidding around!
Now this is the Sandman we all know and love! How ya been?
I've gotta maneuver away from him to take my shot--
--but in these close quarters it's only a matter of time before he--
UNNH!
THOKK!

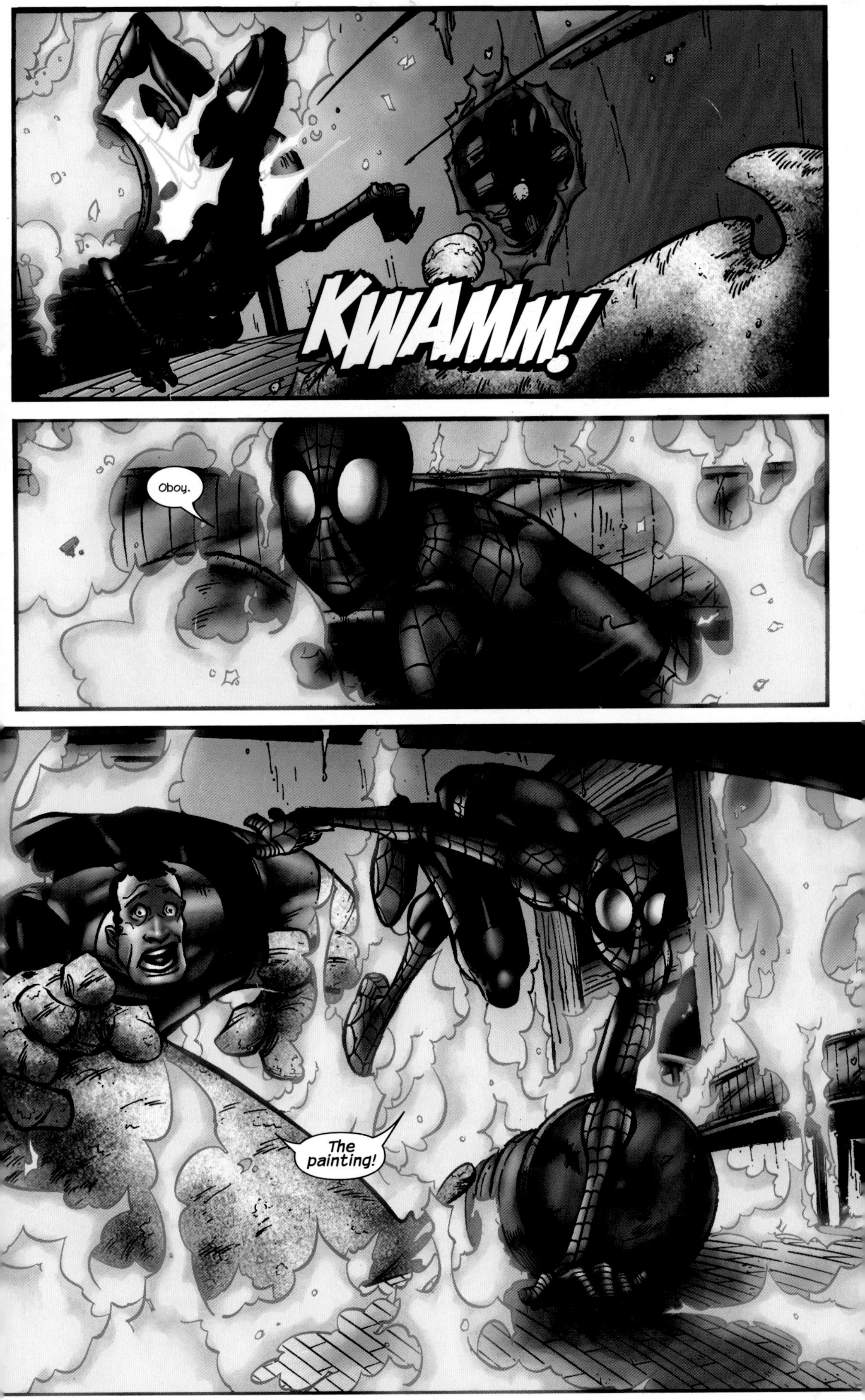
KWAMM!
Oboy.
The painting!

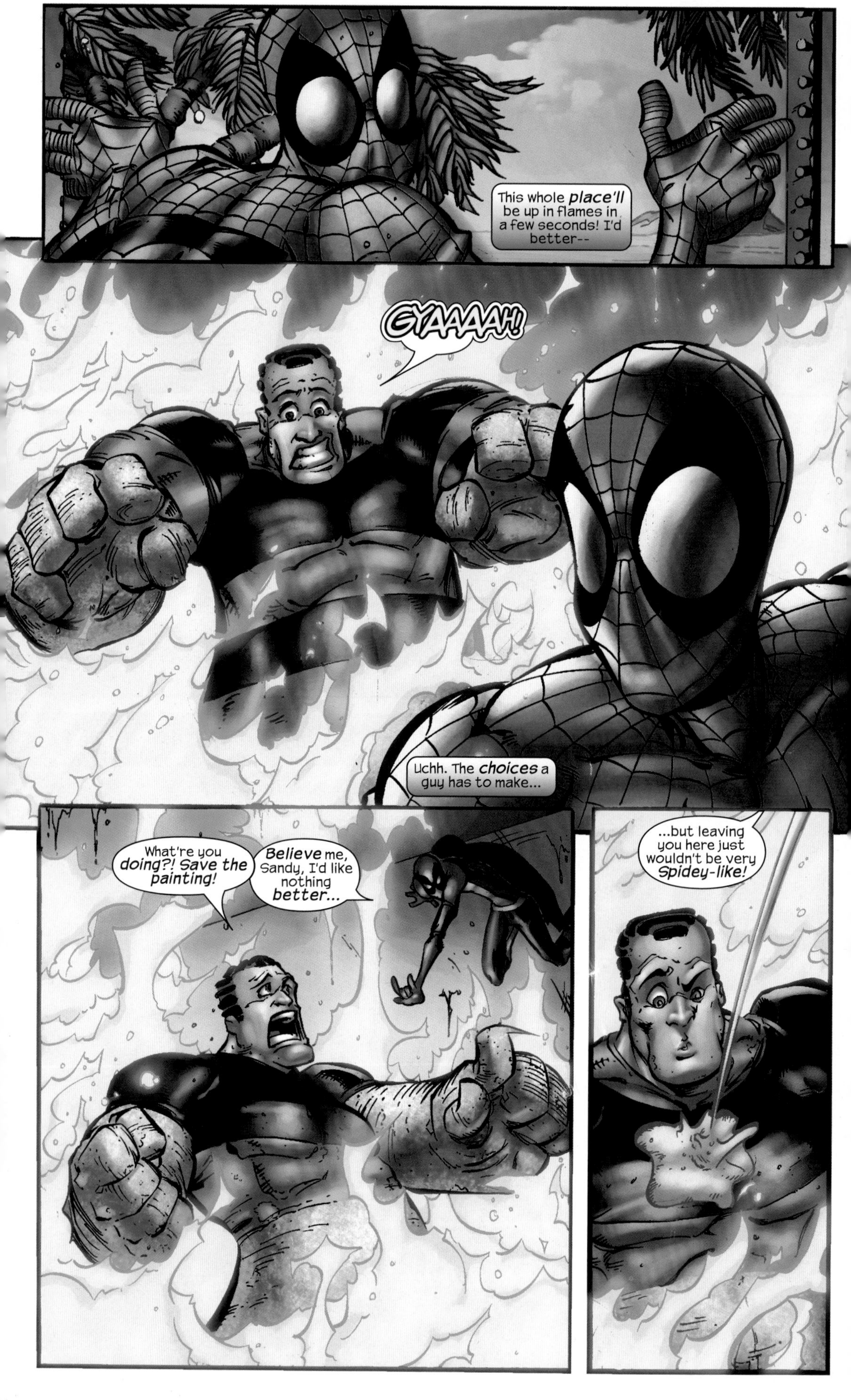
This whole place'll be up in flames in a few seconds! I'd better--
GYAAAAH!
Uchh. The choices a guy has to make...
What're you doing?! Save the painting!
Believe me, Sandy, I'd like nothing better...
...but leaving you here just wouldn't be very Spidey-like!

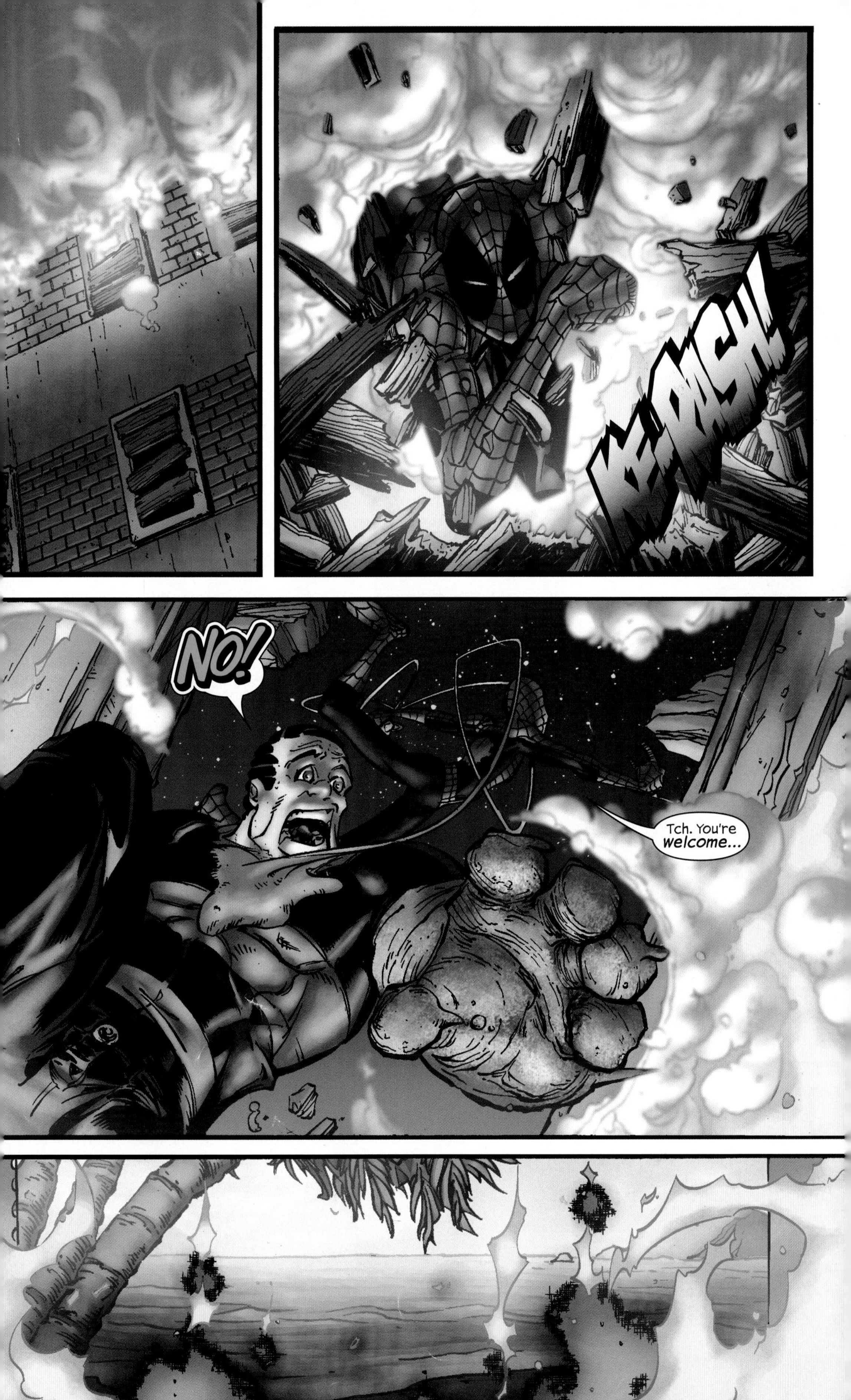
K-RASH!
NO!
Tch. You're welcome...

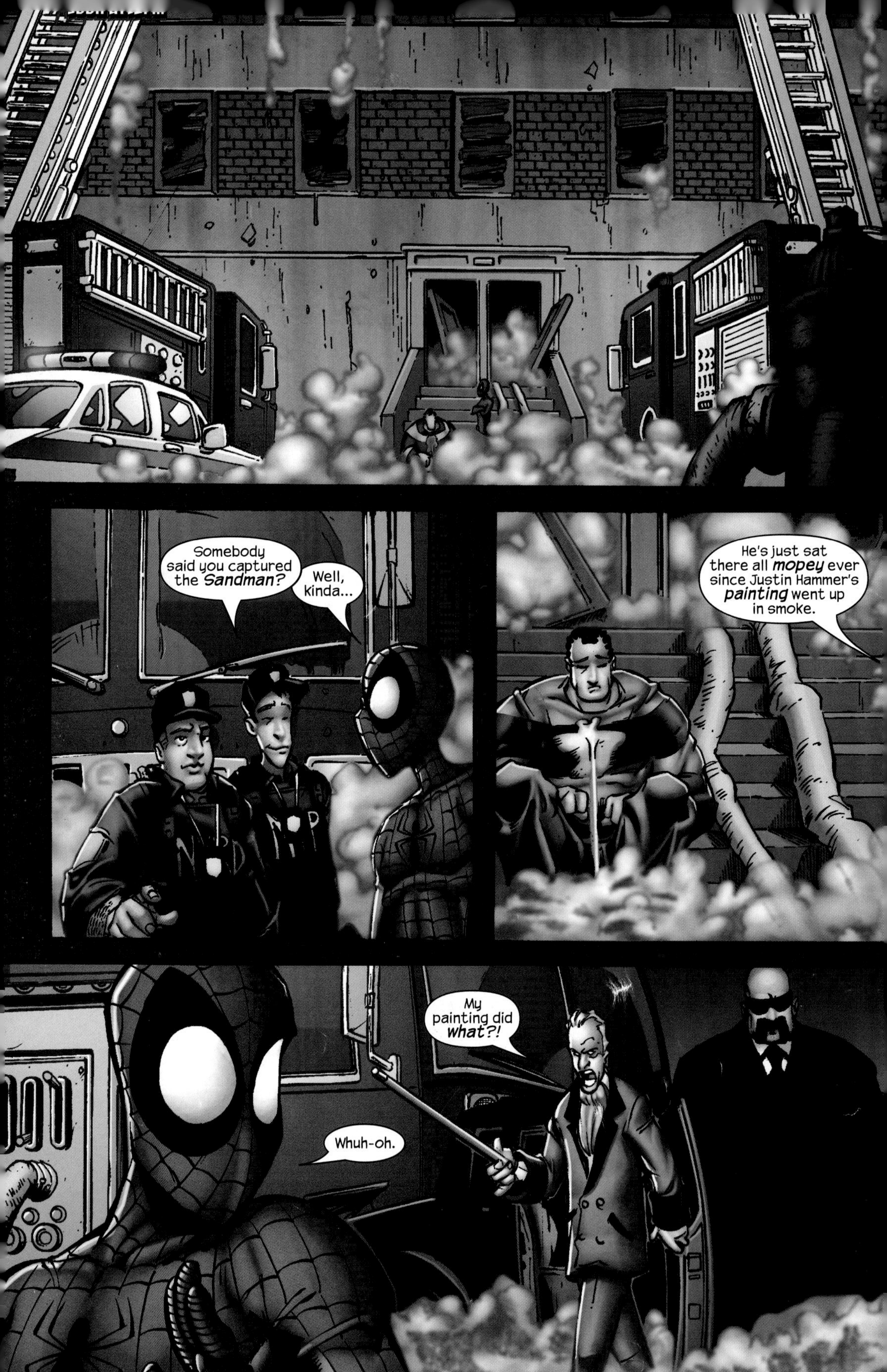
Somebody said you captured the Sandman?
Well, kinda...
He's just sat there all mopey ever since Justin Hammer's painting went up in smoke.
My painting did what?!
Whuh-oh.

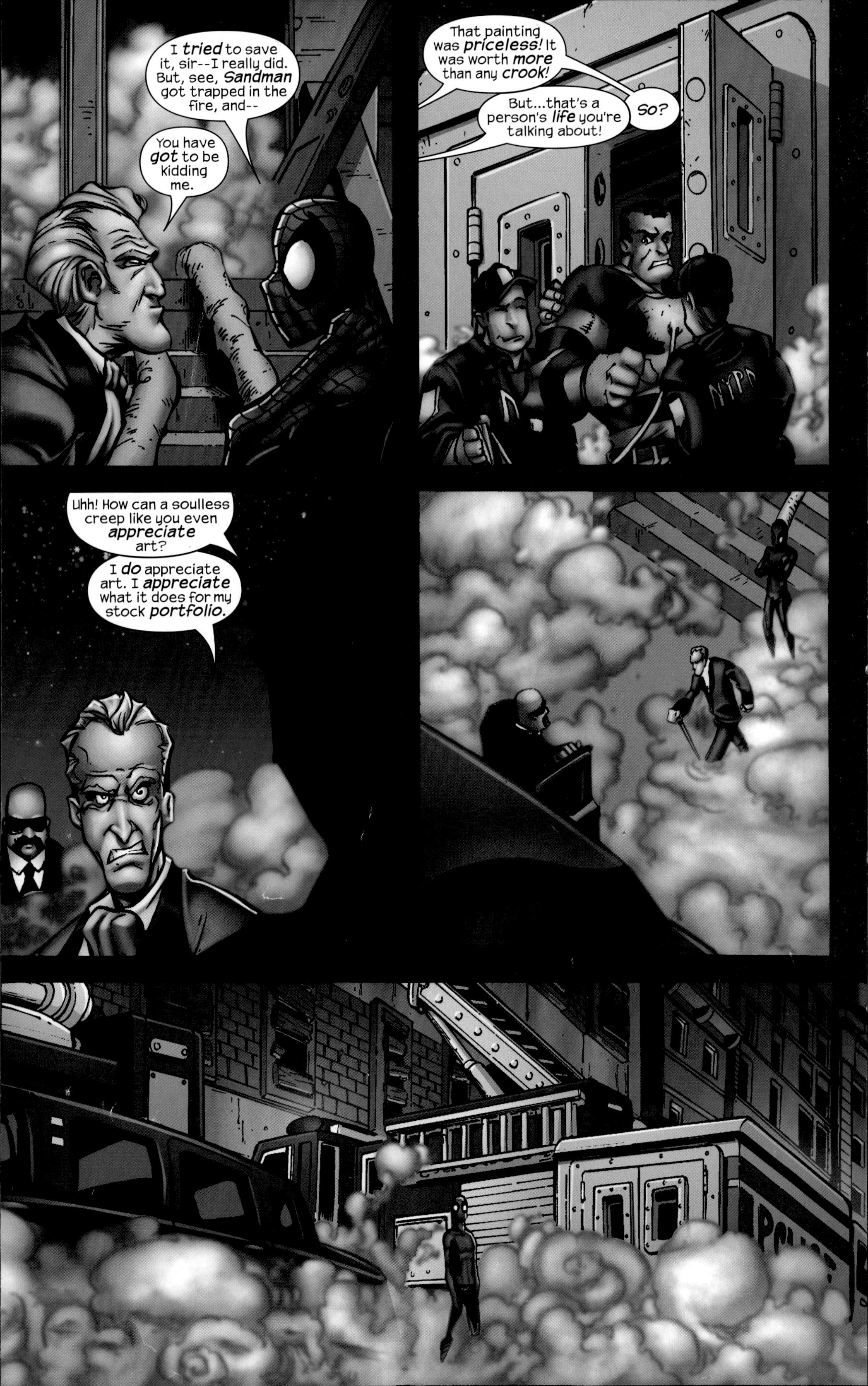

I tried to save it, sir--I really did. But, see, Sandman got trapped in the fire, and--
You have got to be kidding me.
That painting was priceless! It was worth more than any crook!
But...that's a person's life you're talking about!
So?
Uhh! How can a soulless creep like you even appreciate art?
I do appreciate art. I appreciate what it does for my stock portfolio.

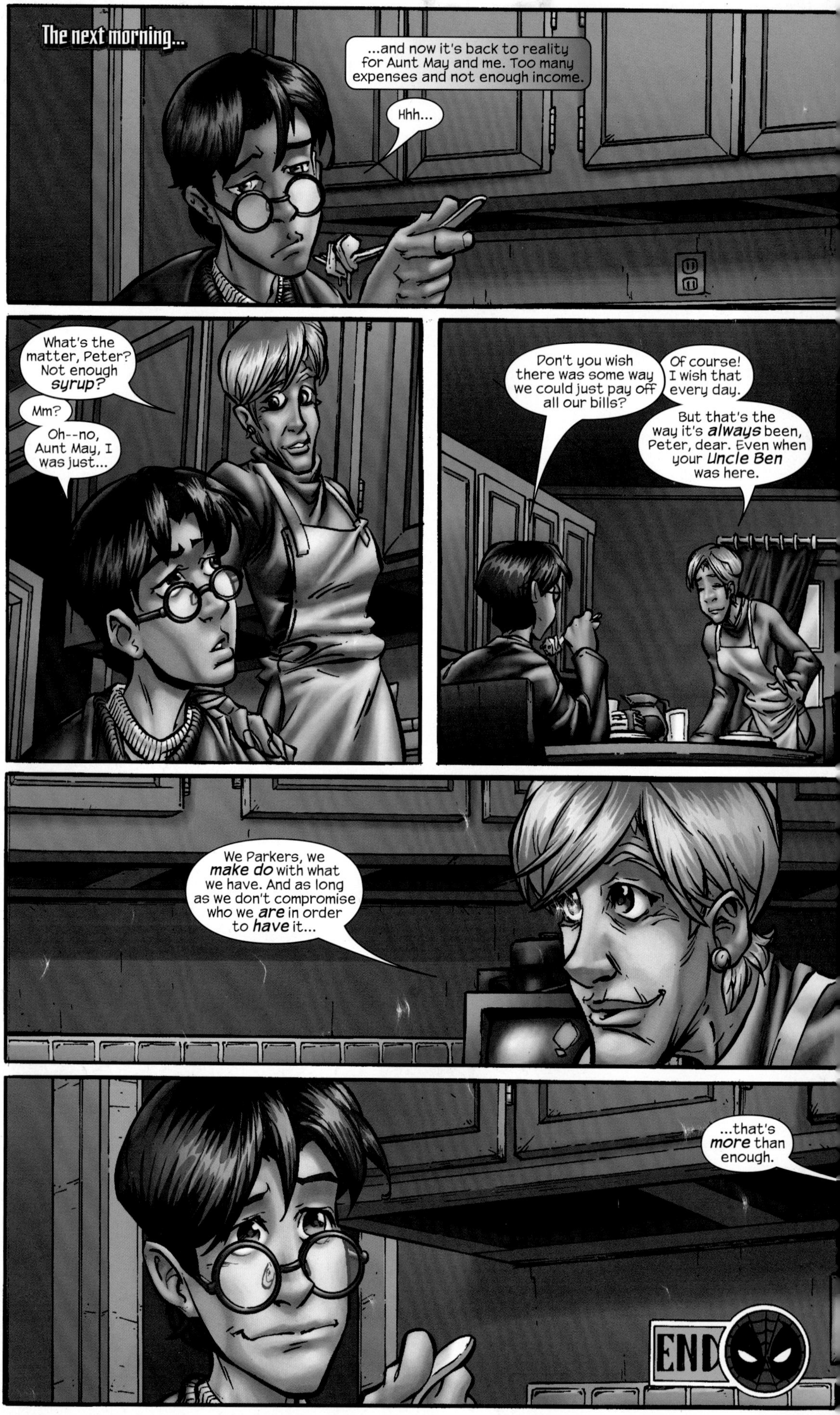
The next morning...
...and now it's back to reality for Aunt May and me. Too many expenses and not enough income.
Hhh...
What's the matter, Peter? Not enough *syrup?*
Mm?
Oh--no, Aunt May, I was just...
Don't you wish there was some way we could just pay off all our bills?
Of course! I wish that every day.
But that's the way it's *always* been, Peter, dear. Even when your *Uncle Ben* was here.
We Parkers, we *make do* with what we have. And as long as we don't compromise who we *are* in order to *have* it...
...that's *more* than enough.
END

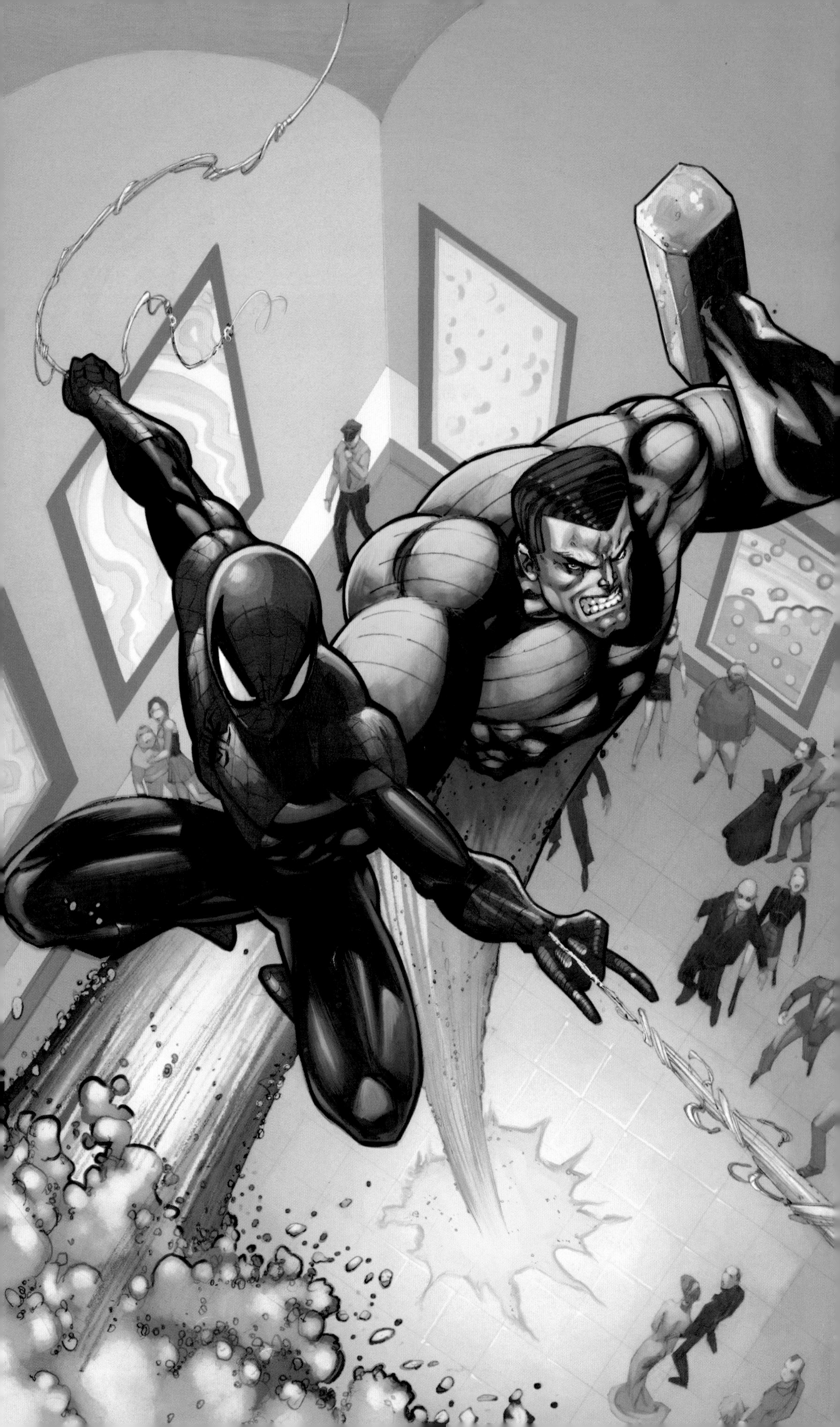